REGRETFUL REVENGE

M.J. PERRY

CONTENTS

COPYRIGHT

1 ~ ZARA

After two years of not setting eyes on Derek, except in her dreams, Zara had expected him to have changed, but he hadn't. Not one bit. The look in his chocolate coloured eyes was full of contempt. She'd thought, or had at least deluded herself into thinking that he'd let her plead her case, or rather her brother's, but it didn't look like he would. In fact, his glare told her he wouldn't, it never left her from the minute his secretary announced her to when she sat in the chair he'd pointed to when she'd walked in his office door. He didn't allow her to speak. As soon as she opened her mouth, he shook his head.

"No." He said in a voice laced with ice. She shivered remembering the last time they'd spoken, and he'd used that voice on her. "Your brother has fucked up and now he will pay for it, along with you, Zara."

Stunned at the venom in his tone she could only stare at him in silence.

He shook his head again. "You can go now."

Like a puppet on a string, she stood feeling

like she was in a bad dream. When her hand closed around the door handle, she turned to face him flinching at the look of disgust on his handsome face. "Why did you agree to meet me?" she asked him.

He shrugged. "I wanted to see if you looked the same as you did two years ago when you threw yourself at me."

Zara turned back to the door and opened it without comment. She didn't want to think about that night.

He spoke again, his words following her out of the door. "You still look innocent, but I see through your act now. I see the manipulative tramp you really are."

Shaking her head, she continued walking, closing the door quietly behind her. Tears filled her eyes, but she refused to let them free. She blinked hard and focused on where she was going. She'd cry later when she could lock herself away in her room, she didn't have the liberty to show weakness right now. Her brother Adrian had made a huge mistake getting himself into debt with Derek's company. Zara was doing a teaching degree and after all her hard work it looked like she would have to give it up and get a full-time job to help pay the mortgage on the house so their mum didn't lose it. Zara didn't mind, well, not much anyway, because the house meant everything to their mum and besides, she could always go back to her degree. What she did mind was that Adrian hadn't told their mum anything. Zara knew it would end up being her who would have to break the news as Adrian was a chicken when it came to telling the truth. Wasn't that why they were in this mess? Adrian had gambled on a ridiculous business plan and practically lost the company their father had built up on his own. Zara didn't believe in happily ever after and with Derek involved it was only a matter of time before the company was no longer theirs.

The lift finally arrived, and she stepped into it sagging against the wall when the doors closed behind her. She refused to let her feelings show on her face. Counting to ten, she let out her breath slowly trying to forget that she had to go home and tell her brother she'd failed. He'd told her she was his last hope, and she'd blown it without even opening her mouth. She'd never understood why Derek hated her so much for telling him she loved him. He'd ripped her apart with his words that night and just now had been no different. He thought she was a tramp; she'd laugh if it didn't hurt so much. She was still a virgin for god's sake, probably the last twenty-four-year-old virgin in the world and Derek thought she slept around. The lift opened, and she checked she had the right floor before stepping off and walking in the direction of the glass covered front doors. Her heels clicked loudly on the tiled floor and she cringed at the sound. She hated heels;

she struggled to walk in them and it took all of her concentration not to stumble and embarrass herself.

When she made it outside and into the sunshine, she sighed in relief. Turning right, she followed the path to her car. She'd been lucky to find a space basically outside the building. Opening the driver's door she slid in and moved her seat back so she could swap her heels for the flats she had there. She couldn't walk in heels safely; there was no way she would attempt to drive in them. Her car was old; her dad had helped her to fix it up after she'd declined his offer of a brand new one. She looked down at her clothes before putting her seat back into position. She'd kept a few clothes from before her dad had died when she'd had to attend events with him, the rest she'd sold and put the money towards her degree, keeping her nest egg topped up. When Adrian had asked her to have the meeting with Derek, she'd found her black suit jacket and matching skirt, which she'd teamed with a pale yellow blouse and black heels. It was almost laughable the care she'd put into her outfit because she could have turned up in her usual attire of jeans, t-shirt and boots for all the good it did her.

She shook her head realising she'd sat in the car too long with the engine running. She didn't want to go home and face Adrian, but she had to. Clicking on her belt, she signalled and pulled out of the space when it was safe, it was time to face the music. Fingers crossed Adrian had been exaggerating when he'd said she was his last hope, there had to be another way to save their father's company. Zara couldn't understand how he'd even got into such a mess; she wasn't sure she wanted to know, but like it or not it was also her mess now. She just prayed there was another way to save the company.

When she made it home, she pulled up outside the house. A few deep breaths later and she felt up to seeing her mum. The act she'd been putting on for her was exhausting and now it would be even more so. They had to keep it from her though. It had been over a year since their dad had died but their mum just didn't seem to be getting over it; her pain was the same as it had been the day it had happened. Her health wasn't as good as it used to be either and she seemed so fragile. It was like she was giving up on life. She wasn't living; she wasn't moving on, she just stayed in the same place, doing the same things each day. It wasn't good for her, but every time Zara broached the subject of her getting a new hobby or joining a club she went all quiet and Zara felt guilty. Adrian was no help, he was too wrapped up in the company and when she asked him to take their mum out, he just pointed out that Zara was a student and had plenty of time to spend with her. If only that were true, sometimes she was so busy she didn't have time to think or even sleep, with work placements and assignments keeping her run ragged. She'd been lucky enough to have an amazing nanna who had left her a trust fund otherwise she didn't know how she would have coped. There was no way she could get a full-time job and study; there just weren't enough hours in the day.

She pulled her keys from the ignition and opened her door. The front door opened before she'd even climbed out and she turned with a smile pasted on her face thinking it would be her mum. She frowned in dismay when she saw it was Adrian instead.

"What are you doing here?" she asked in shock, he hadn't been home before six in nearly a year, even on Saturdays.

"Never mind that Zara, how did it go?"

She looked behind him worried their mum would overhear.

"She's not here; I took her to the salon."

"Oh. It's not really a conversation we should have on the steps." She said as she stepped past him into the house. She could hear his footsteps following her inside. Heading straight for the kitchen seemed like a good idea. She could do with a coffee, well, something stronger would be better, but it was far too early for that.

"Well?" Adrian asked with impatience.

Zara stripped off her jacket and hung it over a

chair, gripping the top of it tightly she finally met his eyes. "He wouldn't help, he didn't even let me speak, he just said no."

Adrian paled.

"Are there no other options?" she asked even though she could see from his face there wasn't.

"No, I've really messed up, Sis."

She pulled out her chair and plonked her behind on it. "I'm sorry."

"Derek was our last hope. I really thought he'd help you. You used to be so close; I thought he'd do it for an old friend."

Zara flinched. It's true, they used to be close, but then she'd mistakenly believed he'd felt more for her, maybe even loved her as she loved him. She'd tried to tell him how she felt. A shiver ran down her spine at the memory. She'd bared her soul to him and he'd pushed her away as if she was a piece of dirt.

"We fell out a long time ago." She said sadly.

"Why the hell didn't you tell me that?" he hissed.

"I thought you knew, and I never thought we would be in this position." She stood up to make the coffee, anything to keep busy. "Do you want a coffee?"

"No, I don't want a fucking coffee, Zara. Shit,

you've really fucked up. I pinned everything on you being able to sweet talk Derek and now we have nothing."

She gasped at his accusation. "I've fucked up?" she asked angrily.

"Don't swear at me."

"I can say what the hell I like when you're placing the blame on me for your mistakes." How dare he tell her it was her fault! In her fury, she didn't see Adrian move until he stood right in front of her.

"It is your fault. You should have brought him round to our thinking, opened your legs if that's what it took to get his agreement."

"You bastard!" she shouted outraged.

"I told you not to swear at me" he shouted back. He raised his hand and slapped her face; her head went back from the force.

She stared at him in shock. The anger faded from his face when he saw her tears. His hand rose again, this time slowly as if he was going to touch her face, and Zara flinched away before he could.

"Zara, I'm so sorry, I don't know what came over me." His voice broke.

She could see he was sorry, but it didn't help her. Her lip throbbed, and she lifted her fingers to it only to hiss in pain. She looked at her fingers and saw blood on them; his ring must have cut her. "You hit me." She whispered. He had never hit her before. He was a happy, easy-going man; she'd never even seen him lose his temper, until now.

"I'll get you some ice." He muttered and without looking at her again he hurried over to the freezer and pulled out some ice. Zara watched him wrap it in a towel. When he walked over and offered it to her she reached out, keeping her distance as much as she could. Placing it on her face she hissed again in pain.

"I've got to go and pick mum up."

"Ok."

"Will you be ok?"

"Yes."

"Zara," he whispered, and she turned to face him for the first time. "I never meant to do that. I'm so sorry."

"I know, but I'm not going to say it's ok because it's not. Things are a lot worse than I thought aren't they?"

He nodded. "More than you can imagine. I've failed you, and mum and dad."

"We'll find a way out of it." she offered, but she wasn't confident they would. "Go and get mum, I'll tell her I walked into the cupboard door. It's not the first time I've done it."

"It will be the first time it's bruised your face."

He said sadly, and she felt his pain, but her face hurt too much for her to acknowledge it. "I won't be long."

"I'll be here." She said and she would be. She breathed a sigh of relief when he left. When she heard his car start and the garage door open, she slid down the cupboard door she was leaning on and burst into tears. She loved her brother; she'd never thought he would raise a hand to her. This on top of her confrontation with Derek was too much for her to handle, but she didn't have the luxury to wallow in self-pity. It was also making her cheek ache more. Her mum could never know that Adrian did this to her, it would break her heart. Zara got up and threw the ice in the sink and finally made herself a cup of coffee. She took it upstairs with her to her bedroom. Stripping out of her suit she pulled on her faded skinny jeans and a pink top then made her way to the mirror. She wasn't sure she wanted to look, but surprisingly it wasn't that bad. Her lip was swollen and her cheek was purple already, but make-up would cover that, she hoped. There was nothing to be done about her lip though. It did look like she'd scratched it on something so the cupboard door lie was as good as the truth; it wasn't like her mum would ever suspect Adrian had hit her.

Turning away from the mirror she grabbed her foundation and tried to cover the bruise. She'd been right, it hid it well. She stuffed all the study books she'd need in her book bag and slipped her feet into her flats before heading downstairs. Once she'd seen her mum and spun her story, she was off to the library, she had assignments to do and even though she knew she wouldn't be able to concentrate, it gave her an excuse to get out of the house.

2 ~ ZARA

As it turned out, Zara and Adrian could act. Their mum didn't suspect a thing, but then, why would she? Zara had no idea how her mum hadn't picked up on the tension between them because although she'd acted like nothing had happened, Zara had been uncomfortable around Adrian. One mistake, a painful one on her part, and it had changed their relationship completely. She couldn't see a way of getting it back to how it was. The trust she had was gone. She'd sat at the table and eaten tea acting as if everything was normal and then she'd excused herself just like she'd planned. Her mum hadn't batted an eyelid because it wasn't unusual for her to disappear, but Adrian had looked so sad.

Now, she was sitting in the corner of the library trying to do research and getting nowhere. She was going to have to give it up so there wasn't much point in her doing it and it wasn't like she could stop thinking about what had happened. She stuck her headphones in and with her music playing quietly she grabbed her laptop and forced herself to do something to occupy her mind. Zara hadn't been sitting down for more than half an hour when a shadow fell over her. Looking up, she found her eyes captured by Derek's. He looked furious. He reached over and gently tugged the headphones out of her ears.

"What the hell happened to your face?"

Zara's fingers moved to her cheek sure he couldn't be talking about that, the foundation had done its job, or so she'd thought. "I walked into a cupboard." She replied while mentally crossing her fingers hoping he would believe her. He searched her face and his lips thinned, she braced for the accusation that she was a liar, but he surprised her by just sighing.

"Let's go and get a coffee."

"I'm ok thanks." She replied quickly. The longer she was with him the more likely she would blurt out the truth. Even with the way, things were between them she knew he'd still comfort her if she fell apart. It made little sense, but she knew it to be true.

"It wasn't a suggestion, Zara."

She raised her eyes to look around the room and saw people were staring. It was because of Derek. He wore a grey designer suit, and it fit his body perfectly, moulding to his broad shoulders, his muscular thighs and toned chest. He was gorgeous, but it wasn't just his good looks that attracted women, he had something else. The way he walked, the way he held himself, he gave off a sense of danger and he projected confidence, which earned him respect from men and appreciation from women. Derek was a mystery as well and didn't women just love that? Zara had always loved him, mainly because of how sweet he'd always been to her, well, until that night.

Looking into his eyes she could see his determination to get her to agree to coffee. If she didn't, he'd have no problem making a scene, he'd also have no qualms about picking her up and throwing her over his shoulder. As much as she wanted him to hold her, she'd be incredibly embarrassed if that happened. She packed her things, sliding everything into her bag. He watched her every move, and it made her clumsy.

"There's a coffee shop just over the road. We can go there." He said.

"Ok." She agreed. Anything for a quiet life.

She picked up her now full bag and was surprised when Derek took it from her. As she stood, he placed his other hand on the small of her back and used it to guide her towards the door. They were both silent on the walk. She was so aware of the warmth of his hand on her and his big body next to hers that it was a struggle to walk in a straight line.

He led her to an empty table when they entered and then went to order their drinks. He didn't ask her what she wanted and with anyone else, it would have annoyed her, but knowing Derek remembered what she liked made some of the coldness recede from her body. After he was served, he walked back to her handing her the drink before sitting down opposite her. She tried not to squirm under his stare and when he didn't speak she broke the silence unable to deal with his scrutiny.

"What do you want Derek?" then it occurred to her. "How did you know where to find me?"

His smile was grim. "I had you followed."

"You had me followed?" she asked in disbelief. "Why?"

"That doesn't matter."

"It doesn't matter?" She almost screeched. How could he say that?

His face hardened. "No, it doesn't matter. I want us to talk about a proposition I have for you."

Still reeling from the fact he'd had her followed she didn't understand for a minute. "A proposition?" she asked him warily as she wrapped her hands around her latte.

"Yes. I will help your brother to keep half of his company."

"Only half?"

"After his monumental fuck-up, you can't expect me to let him keep the whole thing, surely?"

He was right. Adrian didn't deserve a hand out if he would only make the same mistake. "Who would own the other half?" she wasn't sure why she bothered to ask, it was obvious it would be Derek.

"Me, of course," He confirmed. "In fact, I already own it."

"Why would you do this? I mean, it's not out of the goodness of your heart.

"That's where you come in. I want a wife."

She must have misheard him. "You want a wife?"

"Not just any wife, I want you."

"But why?"

"We have unfinished business. I'm feeling my age now and I'm bored with gold-digging women. I want to settle down and have a family."

A picture of him holding a blue-eyed baby entered her mind, and she screwed her eyes up in protest. It had been a dream of hers to have his baby since she'd turned twenty and Derek had comforted her after she'd found out her dad was ill. She'd always thought herself in love with him but that day her feelings had turned into adult love. "You're thirty-five." She pointed out, "Hardly old."

"It's the perfect age to settle down and become a family man."

"You are so matter of fact. What about love

and affection? We have none and I'm pretty sure you hate me. That is not a good way to start a marriage." Did it sound like she was considering it?

"I don't hate you, Zara, I'm just disappointed that you turned out to be no different from the countless women I encounter every day. As for love, it's a fairy-tale. Marriage is based on mutual understanding and lust."

Why did it feel like he'd just slapped her? "My parents had love. It isn't just a fairy-tale."

"Your parents were lucky. It doesn't happen often. Look at your mother now though. Is love really worth it? She's barely alive."

She flinched in pain at having her earlier thoughts spoken out loud.

"My mother is fine."

"Now you're lying. She is not fine and we both know it." Derek was silent for a minute as he studied her face intently. "She has no idea what is going on, does she?"

Zara shook her head.

"Maybe someone should tell her."

His words were like an icy touch on her skin and she shivered. "Is that a threat?"

"That all depends on what your answer is to my proposition."

"It sounds more like blackmail."

He shrugged.

"Spell out what you want from me."

He nodded, "Very well. Marry me and I will gift your brother half of his company."

"And if I don't?"

"If you don't, I will have no choice, but take over the company and kick your brother out. Of course, if that happens you will have to quit your degree and get a full-time job. Your mother will know something is wrong."

"We could explain that I've changed my mind and I'm taking a year off to decide."

"You could and she would believe you but I'll make sure she finds out the truth about how her precious son lost the company her husband built up."

"You're such a bastard." She spat.

Her words amused him and that made her angrier. "I'm a lot of things. You'll find that out before long."

"I need time to think."

"No, you don't. You've already made up your mind. I need the words."

Her teeth clenched at his arrogance. His certainty that she was going to agree made her want to slap his stupid face. He was right though, she was going to agree, she had no other choice. There was no way she'd let her mum hear the truth from him. She'd do anything to protect her. Swallowing hard, she met Derek's eyes. "I'll marry you."

She waited for him to speak, but instead, he stood up and took her hand pulling her to her feet. His arms wrapped around her, his hands settling on her hips and she looked up at him in shock. There was satisfaction in his eyes. When he leaned down towards her, she felt trapped. His lips brushed against hers and when he pulled away, she had to fight the urge to lick her lips.

"What was that for?" she asked in a weak voice.

"Just sealing the deal," He grinned.

"You couldn't have just shaken my hand?" she snapped even as she could feel her body melting into his. Right then, she realised just how hard it was going to be to hide her feelings from him. She'd never stopped loving him even after the way he'd treated her. He seemed to shake off whatever had him holding her tightly against his body and he abruptly let her go, placing a hand on her elbow to steady her, his grip tightened when she tried to shift away. He grabbed her bag from the chair and pulled her out of the coffee shop oblivious to the stares they were getting. Zara blushed as she realised they were all probably thinking her and Derek were rushing off together to be alone. She shivered. He wanted a family which meant she would have to sleep with him. How would she do that and not let words of love flow from her mouth? How was she going to please him when she had no idea what to do? He thought her a woman of the world, boy, was he in for a disappointment. She tried to pull away from him when she realised where he was heading, but his grip tightened even more.

"Where are we going? My car is back there."

"I'm taking you home."

"My home?" she asked warily.

"Yes, Zara, your home, I would never disrespect my bride-to-be by taking her to my home and having my wicked way with her." He gave her a look filled with amusement. "Even if she is far from a virgin bride and could probably teach me a thing or two."

Zara stiffened in hurt. "I can drive myself."

"I know, but I want to be there when you tell your family our happy news."

"I have to tell them now?"

"Oh yes. Now I have your agreement there is nothing standing in my way. We will marry next month."

"Next month?" she squeaked.

"Yes."

That was it. That was all he said. She knew he wouldn't budge, and her shoulders slumped in defeat. Her life was about to change drastically and while it terrified her, she was also excited. She'd dreamt that Derek would be her first, and that was going to happen. She just wished it was because he loved her and not because he wanted some kind of revenge. If she wasn't still in love with him, there was no way she'd be able to sleep with him, she'd run away or something, anything to not let it happen, but stupidly, she did love him. If only he loved her back. How could he want to have sex with her when he didn't love her, didn't even like her? She didn't understand.

"I don't think Adrian will be easily convinced," she said.

"Leave him to me." His voice sent chills down her spine.

He opened the car door, and she climbed in. His hand pulled out the belt, and he leaned over her to buckle her in. She held her breath at the sensations he caused her just from his closeness. When he pulled away, his hand brushed against her breast and she gasped in shock. Her nipples hardened, and she prayed he wouldn't notice. By the smirk on his face, she guessed he had. Again, she wished he couldn't read her as easily as he did.

"We're going to be good together." He said as his hand caressed her burning cheek.

She didn't speak, she couldn't. Instead, her eyes were drawn to his lips. The bottom one slightly fuller than the top one, she watched them curve into a smile showing perfect white teeth. She finally tore her eyes away to meet his.

"Really good together," She heard him mutter as he closed her door and walked round to the driver's side.

She sucked in a breath, she was on fire. No man had ever had such an impact on her body before.

Derek got in the car and settled beside her, turning the key the car purred to life. Zara got more nervous the closer to home they got. The situation was so surreal and now she had to convince Adrian that she was madly in love with Derek and marrying him because she wanted too. It sounded easy, after all, the first part wasn't a lie and as long as she didn't let Adrian get her alone it would be fine because she was a rubbish liar and he'd have the truth out of her in a second.

As soon as the car pulled to a stop outside her house, she found her key in her bag and opened the car door, not waiting for Derek to open it for her. She could see his displeasure, but she ignored it.

"Why the rush, Zara?"

"I want to get it over with."

"I'll do the talking." He said as he gave

her a once over. "I think the latte has left you overwrought."

Was he kidding? He really thought it was the coffee that had her wound up and not him and his ridiculous blackmail? She opened her mouth to call him a jerk, but the front door opened. Derek was holding her keys out for her to take and she realised he'd unlocked the door while his jerkiness had distracted her. She huffed in annoyance, which made him grin, and snatched her keys back. Pushing the door wide she walked in. "I'm home." She called to her mother.

"I'm in the kitchen."

Zara started to walk in the direction but was pulled back by Derek's grip on her hand. She looked at him in question. "We're getting married remember, wouldn't two people in love want to hold hands?"

"Sure, but I'd much rather hit you." She glared at him.

"You'd only do it once."

Reluctantly she stopped trying to tug her hand free and led him to the kitchen. Her mum turned at their footsteps and she gasped in delight as she saw Derek. Quickly drying her hands on a towel she hurried over to him and wrapped her arms around him. He didn't let go of Zara's hand as he wrapped an arm around her mother, hugging her back.

"It's been so long, Derek. Sit down, I'll put the kettle on, and you can tell me all about what you've been up to."

Her happiness at seeing him wasn't a surprise to Zara; her mum had always thought the world of him and she'd been upset when he'd stopped visiting.

"I'll make the drinks and you two can catch up." Zara offered, and she caught Derek's amused glance. He knew she was putting off telling her mum the news, but amazingly, he was letting her get away with it. He finally let go of her hand after giving it a squeeze and she left them at the table.

The front door opened a few minutes later, and Zara nearly spilt her coffee. Derek didn't miss her reaction and his lips thinned. She'd figured he'd put it down to nerves, but one look at his furious face and she thought he might know that Adrian had hit her.

"Ma," Adrian called.

"We're in the kitchen," she called back.

He couldn't have missed the Jag parked outside the house, he must know they had a visitor, but by the look on his face, he'd had no clue it was Derek. His eyes flew to Zara's in shock and she shook her head to indicate that their mum didn't know anything.

"Look who came for a visit. It's been such a long time." Their mum exclaimed.

Adrian swallowed hard before looking at Derek. "Yes, it has. How are you?"

"Fine, well, more than fine, actually," Derek replied. He held out a hand to Zara, and she placed hers in it, her heart banging in her throat. "We have some great news."

"Great news?" her mum asked excitedly looking at their joined hands and Derek's smile. Zara eyes, however, were on her brother and he looked worried.

"I asked Zara to be my wife, and she said yes."

Zara forced a smile to her lips. "Isn't it brilliant?" She exclaimed in what she hoped was a giddy voice. She didn't think she'd succeeded if Derek's face was anything to go by.

"You're getting married?" Adrian asked her slowly.

"We are. Are you happy for us?" Derek asked. Was Zara the only one to hear the taunt in his voice?

"Once I've spoken to my sister alone, I'll answer that."

Oh god. Panic hit her. She didn't want to be alone with him so he could question her and she still felt uncomfortable after earlier. Derek was already shaking his head. "I'm not letting her out of my sight, not when I've only just got her back." Derek raised a hand to her chin. "Go and pack some things for the next couple of days. We'll come back for the rest soon."

"Pack?"

"You agreed to move in with me remember?"

She'd done no such thing, and he knew it. He'd backed her into a corner because she couldn't say no, not with Adrian watching them like a hawk. She looked past Derek at her brother and saw he wasn't quite buying it. Derek hadn't mentioned moving in, but it would be stupid of her not to realise it would happen when she was marrying him. Maybe she'd be able to get him to soften towards her before their big day.

She smiled softly. "I'll go now."

"And I'll come with you. I don't want you lifting anything heavy."

Her mum gasped and Zara had actually forgotten she was there she'd been so quiet. "Are you pregnant Zara?"

Zara blushed brightly looking at Derek to see him grin before he answered for her. "Not yet, but we don't want to wait too long to start a family. Do we sweetheart?"

While her mum was cooing about babies, Adrian muttered something that had Derek stiffening; she felt the tension in the room go up a notch.

"Come on, then." She grabbed Derek's arm, "let's go pack." He let her lead him upstairs to her room. She hesitated at the door not sure if she wanted him in her space but she didn't exactly have a choice. He didn't pay much attention to anything he just walked over to her bed and sat down. He looked at her and his serious expression had her worried.

"Did your brother ask you to meet with me?"

She frowned at the question. "Yes, he did."

"What was his reaction when you told him I wouldn't help?"

"He was upset."

Derek looked pointedly at her lip. "How upset?"

A look of guilt crossed her face; she'd never been very good at hiding her feelings from him. He suddenly grabbed her by the shoulders and she squeaked in surprise.

"Did he hit you?"

She shook her head knowing she couldn't lie to him but she didn't want to admit the truth. He pulled her into the warmth of his body and his arms wrapped around her tightly. She turned her head and rested her cheek against his chest. His heart beat strong and steady in her ear and it made her feel safe. His comfort confused her, and she reluctantly shifted in his arms, he slowly loosened his hold as if he couldn't bear to let her go.

"I need to pack." She announced. Anything to get away from his touch.

He studied her face for a moment and when he dropped his gaze, it was a relief to look away from him. She took her bag from the back of the wardrobe and packed some clothes. Next, she went to the bathroom and grabbed her toothbrush and toiletries. Derek was still standing where she'd left him when she returned.

"Ready?" she asked him and he seemed to shake himself before taking the bag from her hands. She followed him to the door, and he held it open letting her go down the stairs first. Her mum was still smiling and despite everything, it made Zara smile too. She hadn't seen her mum this happy since her dad had been alive.

"Adrian apologises, but he had to head out." Her mum said.

Zara hid her relief. "Ok, I'll speak to him soon."

"He'll come round. He's just worried you're rushing into things."

"We aren't, Mum."

She smiled. "I can see you're happy."

"Yes, completely," Luckily, her mum was too

caught up in her own happiness to see Zara was lying through her teeth.

"You've always loved him, Honey. I'm glad you've found a way back to each other."

Blushing, Zara turned to see Derek standing in the doorway. He'd put her bag by the front door and she hoped he hadn't heard what had been said. His expression told her otherwise, she could see he didn't believe her mum's words. She wasn't sure if that was a good thing or not. Deciding to pretend the conversation hadn't happened she smiled at her mum. "We need to go, but I'll ring you tomorrow."

"Ok, baby girl."

Zara leaned in and kissed her cheek. "Love you, Ma."

"Love you too, always."

"Bye Derek." Her mum did a girly wave and Zara giggled.

"Bye Mrs Moore."

"Oh," she tutted at him. "You're going to be part of the family, call me Marge."

"Bye, Mum," Zara said as she urged Derek out of the door. He didn't speak. It made her nervous wondering what was going on in his head. She didn't have to wonder long.

"Adrian looked guilty." He said into the silence.

"He hasn't told our mum anything; it worried him that you had, that's all." It wasn't a complete lie.

"Hmm, well, he will need to think of something to tell her as he only owns half the company now."

"I'm sure my mum will think it's great that you own the other half."

"I'm sure she will. She seemed thrilled for us. I guess you didn't tell her what you did?"

What she did? He meant the night she'd practically thrown herself at him, opened her heart to him and told him she loved him. The same night he'd thrown her away from him in disgust and told her she was the last woman in the world he would ever be with. "No." she whispered. Her cheeks warmed from the remembered humiliation.

"I'm not surprised. She doesn't need to know what a gold-digging slut you are."

"I can't believe you just said that." She whispered her hurt clear in her voice.

"Why not Zara? It's the truth, isn't it?"

She shook her head. "I never wanted your money."

"No?" he said sarcastically.

"No, I…" she trailed off. She was going to say that she'd loved him, but what was the point. He wouldn't believe her.

"You loved me?" he finished for her.

She turned away. "What's the point in talking about this? You've already made up your mind about me and you won't change it."

"You're right. I won't change my mind. I know the truth because the same night you decided you were in love with me, your brother asked me for a loan because he'd had a business idea which was going to net him millions, if only he had my backing." He shook his head. "What was the plan? Throw your sweet body at me to sweeten the deal?"

"What?" she asked in shock.

"Don't pretend you didn't know Zara, I wasn't born yesterday."

"But I knew nothing about that." She protested. Her bloody brother had a lot to answer for.

"Enough!" he shouted, and she flinched. "We are not discussing this anymore."

"But-"

"No, no buts, Zara. If you bring up the past again, our deal is off."

She nodded. Her eyes filled with tears and she turned away so he wouldn't see. He hadn't even given her the chance to defend herself. His allegations hurt her, but what hurt the most was that he believed she would offer her body so cheaply.

"Why are you forcing me to marry you if you think so badly of me?" she asked tearfully. She could feel his stare on her but she didn't turn to face him.

"Ever since that night you almost bared yourself to me I've wondered what you'd be like in bed and now I'm going to find out."

It was on the tip of her tongue to tell him she was a virgin, but he'd only call her a liar. He was in for a surprise. She didn't bother to answer, what could she say to that.

"Think yourself lucky I'm making you my wife and not my mistress." He said into the silence.

She clenched her fists. Being his mistress would be embarrassing but being his wife would be hell. She would be tied to a man who despised her, and she had to give him a child. She'd always wanted to marry Derek, but not like this. Pretending to be happy was going to be hard. Maybe she should try to talk him into letting her be his mistress, at least he'd let her go once he got bored with her. Then, she could try to move on from him.

Right now though, she was trapped, and that was terrifying.

3 ~ ZARA

When they pulled up outside Derek's house Zara took a deep breath not wanting to let him see how nervous she was. The truth was she was scared. He turned the key and the car went silent. She heard a click and turned to watch the large brown gates at the end of the driveway shut the world out.

Derek released his belt and got out. She'd just released hers when he opened her door. Maybe he thought she was going to bolt because he put his hand out for her. She reluctantly placed hers in it and let him help her out of the car. He closed her door and led her to the boot, grabbing her bag and closing the boot with a bang. The lights flashed indicating he'd locked the car before he led her up the steps to the house.

Holy crap it was pretty. She instantly loved it on sight and when he unlocked the door and turned the alarm off she fell in love with it even more. It was old-fashioned with solid pine furniture, beige sofas and tiled floors. It made her hate Derek for having such a gorgeous house when he was such a jerk.

"I'll show you to our room." He said into the silence.

She only nodded not wanting to think too much on his words.

He carried her bag for her and placed it on the bed when they entered. The bed dominated the entire room, she wasn't sure what size it was, but it made the other furniture look doll sized.

"Why don't you have a shower?"

"Ok." She said warily.

"I have some work to do."

Hiding her relief, she walked to the bed and opened her bag. Taking what she needed out of it, she headed to the en-suite. The shower was separate from the bath and it had jets all over the walls, she knew it would be heaven to use. She turned the water on and quickly stripped off, placing her toiletries within reach, she climbed in and sighed with delight. Once she'd washed and scrubbed every inch of herself she washed her hair and got out. At least if life was hell, she had an amazing shower to use, she would just hide in there. Drying herself, she quickly pulled on her pyjamas and dried her hair pulling it into a loose ponytail. She took a look at her face in the mirror and winced at the bruise. It was darker now; tomorrow it would be harder to hide. She wondered what Derek would say when he saw it. Bracing herself, she opened the bathroom door and found him sitting on his bed.

"Fuck, Zara, I want to kill your brother." He growled.

She swallowed. "He didn't mean it."

"He hit you and left a bruise. Believe me, he may be sorry, but he meant to hurt you at the time."

She knew that. It's why it hurt so much.

He shook his head and the concern she'd thought had been there disappeared. "Are you on the pill?"

She shook her head.

"Surely an experienced woman like yourself should be. What's the matter, did you get sick of the party life?"

It was like he'd punched her, she nearly doubled over from the pain. He knew he'd hurt her, she couldn't hide it from him. "If you think I'm so experienced why don't you let me work off the debt on my back instead of forcing me to be your wife?" she exploded in anger.

His expression turned to ice. "If that's what you want Zara, it can be arranged."

She raised her eyes to his warily. "What do you mean?"

Instead of answering, he pointed to the floor in front of him. "Come here."

She shook her head.

"Now, Zara, don't make me come to you."

She swallowed back her fear and hesitantly took a step and then another until she reached him. His eyes were blank, and she shivered.

"Kneel." He ordered in a cold voice.

She did as he said.

"If you'd rather be my mistress, then you can act like it."

Tears pricked her eyes, and she quickly blinked them away.

"Open my belt."

She reached up to undo the buckle feeling sick to her stomach. Her tears fell silently down her cheeks and she kept her face hidden so he wouldn't see.

"Open my button and undo the zip." He ordered once the belt was open.

Her hands shook as once again she reached up and did as he said. Her fingers fumbled on the button before she managed to pull it free, the zip was easy and she slid it down.

"Pull my trousers down." He ordered.

She sniffed. Gripping the waistband, she pulled them and they came down easily enough until he was stood in just his underwear. Fisting her hands on her lap she waited for his next order but it didn't come. Instead, she heard him growl and suddenly he was kneeling in front of her. He lifted her chin with a finger until she was looking at his tormented face.

"Zara, forgive me." He whispered his voice full of regret. Her eyes widened in shock and then she closed them. A lone tear fell from her eye and he brushed it away softly.

"Open your eyes."

She did, curious at the soft tone he'd used.

"I am so sorry for acting that way."

"It's ok."

"No, it's not. It's no more ok than Adrian hitting you."

"Why did you do it?" she whispered.

"I got so angry at the thought of you with other men."

"I've never been with other men." She admitted. She bit her lip waiting for his reaction.

He studied her face and then hung his head. "I believe you."

"You do? But why?"

"I've just come to the conclusion that I'm a fucking idiot." He got up and pulled her to her feet. "You can have this bed tonight; I'll sleep in the spare room."

"Ok." She said confused.

He sighed. "I will never treat you the way I just have again. I won't touch you unless you ask me to."

Was that disappointment she felt? "What about the deal, will I be your mistress?"

"Never will you be my mistress, Zara. The deal is for you to be my wife and that hasn't changed."

"Ok." What else could she say?

"Goodnight." He said, and he walked out the door, closing it with a quiet snap.

Zara sank to the floor. "What the hell just happened?" she whispered.

4 ~ ZARA

A knock at the door woke Zara from a fitful sleep and she sat up rubbing her eyes.

"Zara?" Derek called.

"Yes?" she croaked holding the duvet over herself.

"I have to go to the office for a couple of hours. Will you be ok?"

"I'll be fine."

"I've put the coffee on ready for you."

"Thanks."

He hesitated before answering. "I remember how much you love coffee in the morning."

She smiled to herself. He was like a different person, the shutters had fallen away.

"If I remember rightly, you do too. Didn't you nearly fire someone because they broke the coffee machine in your office?"

He chuckled, and the sound brought tears to

her eyes. She'd missed this Derek.

"That's just a rumour. You shouldn't believe everything you hear, babe."

Babe? Probably just a slip of the tongue.

"I've got to go. When I get back we can go out for lunch if you'd like?"

"I'd like that." She called.

"Great. Bye Zara."

"Bye Derek." She called and pulled the duvet over her head. She had to get up she had things to do, or did she? If he was only going to be gone a couple of hours, she could have a long shower, get dressed, drink coffee and have her breakfast at a leisurely pace. Taking her time sounded like heaven compared to how she usually did it all in a rush. That's what she would do, first though, she tried to make sense of Derek's attitude change. It was as if they'd gone back in time to before she'd made a fool of herself and she couldn't understand why.

Last night had been atrocious, she'd never get over him treating her like that but if that was the reason for the change in him now she was glad it had happened. She hoped she could make him see that she'd never been in on any plan with her brother. Adrian was a total screw up. Thinking of him reminded her of her face and she reached up to touch it. It hurt, it was sore and it would probably be a struggle to cover it, but she'd try her best. She didn't want pitying looks or questions about how she'd done it because then she'd have to tell more lies.

Throwing off the duvet, she climbed out of bed and headed to the bathroom. She winced when she saw her reflection in the mirror, yep, she'd been right, it would be tough to cover it up. There was a purple bruise all over one side of her cheek. At least her lip had gone down a bit. She'd shower, drink coffee and then try her best with her foundation.

5 ~ DEREK

Derek was staring out of his office window not really seeing anything. His thoughts were in turmoil. He'd judged Zara wrong, treated her like dirt and last night he'd almost forced her. What was wrong with him? Jealously was a huge part of it, but mostly he was hurt that she would use her body to help her brother seal a deal, except, she hadn't done that. He knew that now, and they'd lost so much time. He would not have pushed her away that night, he would have taken her up on her offer and he wouldn't have let her go. Fuck, he loved her, he always had and revenge had seemed like the best way to get her out of his system. Wasn't he stupid? The only thing it had done was to make him see that he was a fucking idiot. He knew she wasn't like that, her past behaviour showed him that, but he'd chosen to believe the worst and look where that had got them. He was going to make everything better for her, but first, he had a score to settle. A knock at the door had him turning to face it. "Come in," he called.

The door opened and a sombre looking Adrian

walked in.

"You wanted to see me?" Adrian asked.

"Yes, we have things to discuss." Derek moved from behind his desk and towards Adrian.

When he shut the door Derek swung his fist and hit Adrian square in the face. Adrian landed on his behind on the floor, holding his face he sat there stunned for a minute.

"I deserved that." He said quietly. "She told you?"

"Not really. It wasn't hard to work out. You will never touch your sister again, if you do, I will rip you apart."

Adrian nodded and got to his feet. "I didn't mean to hurt her; I don't know why I did it." He sat in one of the chairs and put his head in his hands.

Derek shook his head. He didn't feel any pity for him, but he could see he was sorry. Zara had promised he'd never laid a finger on her before and Derek believed her, but it didn't make it ok. He looked down at his knuckles and saw they were swollen. A bruise would form on there he was sure but damn it had felt good punching him.

"Right," He said. "Whatever I say in this room stays between us. Is that clear?"

"Yes." Adrian agreed.

"Good. I want you to know that I think you

are a fuck up and although I've decided to let you keep half the company, you will not have any access to money or be able to make any decisions without consulting me first. Is that clear?"

Adrian looked shocked. "Why would you do that?"

"Because I love your sister and even though you've hurt her and broke her trust, she still wouldn't want me to destroy you like I really want to do."

"I love my sister."

"I know and that's the only reason I haven't had you disposed of."

Adrian bit his lip. "You love her?"

"Yes."

"She said you'd fallen out."

"Again, that was your fault. You let me think Zara would like it very much if I'd have given you that loan you so desperately needed."

Adrian paled. "I'm the reason you broke her heart?"

"There was a misunderstanding, and I pushed her away. I'm going to make up for it now. So are you."

"I'll do anything; I never wanted any of this. I thought I was taking the company into the twenty-first century."

"Instead, you lost it to me. You're lucky it wasn't to someone else."

"I'm thankful for that, trust me."

"I don't trust you. You will need to earn that. Bottom line, I'm going to marry Zara. You are going to keep half of your company and everyone is going to live happily ever after."

"Ok."

"Zara is going to be my wife by the end of the month."

"That doesn't leave a lot of time to arrange it."

"I have everything in place, don't worry about that. She will want you to walk her down the aisle."

"It would be an honour to do it."

"Good. She's unsure of you after what you did. She won't want to be around you yet, she needs time."

"I understand."

"Good. You can go back to work now."

Adrian nodded and rose from his chair. "I'll see you later."

"I won't be at the meeting. I'm going home." Derek said.

"Oh, ok. I'll tell them you won't be available

then." Adrian said.

"I would appreciate that."

"No problem. Bye." Adrian said as he left the room.

Derek sighed. That had gone well. He'd wanted to punch him some more, but that wasn't the solution to the situation. He tidied up his desk and turned his laptop off. For the first time in years he was going home, and he wasn't coming back until the morning. He'd got his secretary to cancel all his meetings. He had some making up to do with Zara and he intended on starting now. He was going to wine her, dine her and show her he was the same man from before, the one she'd claimed to love. Hopefully, he could earn that love back. He wanted her to be his wife because she loved him, not because he was forcing her.

6 ~ZARA

When Derek walked in Zara was sat in the kitchen drinking her second cup of coffee. She thought she'd managed to cover the bruise, but by the look on his face, she hadn't succeeded.

"Fuck, I want to go and kill him." He growled.

Zara jumped up in alarm. It actually looked like he was going to walk out the door.

"It's fine, I'm fine." She said as she walked over to him stopping a couple of inches in front of him. His swollen knuckles caught her eye, and she gasped. "What have you done?" she asked as she gently picked up his hand to examine it.

"I punched Adrian."

"Oh Derek, you shouldn't have." She said sadly.

"He hit you." He hissed.

"Hitting him doesn't make it all better."

"It felt really good though."

She smiled at his childish grin. "Is everything ok between you now?"

"Things will never be ok between us, but as he's your brother and you clearly want him in our lives, I'll deal with him politely when I have to."

She nodded. "Thank you. It means a lot that you would do that."

"I know. I'm going to go and change and then we're going for a drive."

"Ok, I'd like that. Judging from your reaction to my face the bruise must be obvious so I'd rather stay away from people. I don't want anyone to think you did this."

"I don't care what people think, you shouldn't either."

"I do care. Because of who you are the press would have a field day writing about you. I don't want you to lose business."

He shook his head. "After what I've done to you, I can't believe you're worried about me."

She paused before answering, not wanting to give herself away. "I care about you. You were once my friend."

"Friend, right," he said in an odd voice. "Wait here and I'll get ready."

"Ok." She went to sit back down. Picking up her coffee; she took a sip pondering his reaction to her words. Did he want another declaration of love? After the last time she'd done that and he'd humiliated her there was no way she would put herself out there like that again. She may love him but she would never tell him unless he said the words first, and she didn't think that was likely to happen.

Derek came back and his footsteps made her jump.

"Ready, Zara?"

"Yes, I'll just rinse my cup."

"Do it later, babe."

She raised her eyebrows. That couldn't have been a slip of the tongue, surely? Putting her cup in the sink, she grabbed her bag from where she'd put it on the side and took her coat from the back of the chair. Derek took it from her and helped her into it, his hands tightened on her shoulders and she fought a shiver at his strength. He surprised her by linking their hands and tugging her towards the front door and they walked out into the sunshine. Derek locked the door behind them and then led her to his car. She saw her car parked next to it.

"How did my car get here?"

"I had someone pick it up this morning."

"Oh, thanks."

"You're not keeping it."

"What?" she stopped walking and tried to tug her hand free.

"Baby, it's old and unreliable. You need something safe to drive."

"I'm not getting rid of it." She said stubbornly.

"And I don't expect you to."

"You don't?"

"No. I know how much it means to you. There is room in the garage for it you just have to promise me you won't drive it anymore."

"I don't like your bossiness."

"You'll get used to it."

"I don't think I will."

"You'll learn to live with it, then." He grinned.

That grin made her toes curl. She started walking again determined not to let him see her reaction to him. He opened the car door with a grin on his handsome face. She climbed in and he closed the door making his way to her side.

"I have a little surprise for you." He said as he sat down.

"You do?" she said excitedly.

"Don't ask me anything, I won't tell you a thing."

She pouted.

"You'll find out in about ten minutes."

She smiled. "I can't wait."

****

Ten minutes felt more like ten hours, but finally, they pulled up outside a building. It looked like a restaurant, but it had a closed sign hanging in the window. Derek opened her door and helped her out. He led her towards the building and gave a swift knock to the window. The door opened almost immediately.

"Come in, come in." A short, stout man exclaimed as he held the door open wider for them.

Derek clapped the man on the back in a friendly greeting. "Thank you for doing this, Antonio."

"No, no thanks needed. I love, love." He grinned.

Bemused, Zara let herself be herded into the kitchen and up some stairs. Derek opened the door at the top and she gasped.

"It's beautiful." She whispered.

"Come and have a proper look," Derek said as he pulled her through the doorway and onto the roof.

Pink roses littered the floor making a path towards a table decorated with flickering candles. As she got closer, she saw a jewellery box.

Derek let go of her hand and she stood still watching him as he made his way to the table. He picked up the box and made his way back to her taking her hand in his.

"Zara, will you marry me?"

"I've already said yes." She said confused at the romantic gesture.

"Yes, but that was because I was forcing you."

"And now you're not?"

He shook his head. "Today is all about us if you want that?"

"I do." She whispered.

"So, will you be my wife?"

"Oh, yes."

He sighed in relief. "You've made me a happy man." He pulled her into a quick hug before letting her go and taking the ring from the box. "Let's make this official." He said as he slid the ring on her finger.

"It's a rose." She said as she got a better look at it.

"Your favourite flower."

"You remembered."

"I remember everything."

Zara was confused. She wanted his words and actions to be real, and she thought they might be, but a part of her was worried it was all to do with his revenge plan. Why had he suddenly had a change of heart? She was afraid to ask him, but she had to know, she couldn't go on always wondering if any minute he was going to pull the rug from under her.

"Derek?"

"Yes?"

"What does all this mean?"

"The proposal?"

"Yes."

"It's a fresh start for us."

She raised her eyebrows.

"After last night I can understand you being wary of me, but I promise you are safe with me. Do you believe that?"

"I think I do." She said surprising even herself.

"Trust me."

"I'll try."

"I know you aren't who I accused you of being and I'm sorry I treated you the way I did. I really regret my actions."

He sounded stuffy, and she realised that apologising was something he didn't do very often if at all. He didn't ever think he was wrong.

"I forgive you."

"You do?"

"Yes, but it will be harder to forgive my brother." She shook her head sadly. "He actually insinuated that I was happy to give you my body in exchange for your help?"

"He pretty much told me that by helping him you would be very grateful."

"Oh god, no wonder you didn't believe what I was saying." She hung her head.

"Zara, look at me."

She lifted her head and met his eyes.

"I don't think that now." His hand lifted and gripped her chin firmly between his fingers. She couldn't look away from him. Trapped in his gaze, her breath hitched. He heard it and smiled. It wasn't a sexy smile or even the one she'd become used to, no, this smile was pure happiness and it was reflected in his eyes. She smiled back.

"I love you." He told her and she believed him. Her eyes blurred.

"I love you too."

"I know. I've always known, even when I didn't want to believe it. You wear your heart on your sleeve."

"Oh."

"Even when I was being a dick, I knew you loved me, I knew I loved you, but I was hurt."

"It's truly all behind us now? No more revenge?"

"No more revenge, Zara, I promise."

"Good. Can I tell you a secret?"

"You can tell me anything."

"I'd like to marry you in a small ceremony with just our close friends and family."

"Really?"

She nodded.

"You can have that if it's what you really want."

"You're not upset?"

"It's about you and me, no one else."

"I'm glad. I know you're important and have a lot of friends. I don't want to upset anyone, but I want our wedding to be about us."

"And it will be. What about Vegas?"

"What about it?"

"Shall we get married there?"

"Married in Vegas?"

"Yes."

"But that will cost a fortune." She exclaimed.

"Zara, I'm filthy rich or had you forgotten?"

She grinned. "I didn't realise you were that

rich."

"Well, I am. You want to get married in Vegas so we will. I'll get my secretary Molly to make the arrangements. We can take my private jet."

"Holy crap," She whispered.

"Is that a yes?" he laughed.

"Yes, that's a yes." She laughed with him. "Oh."

"What's wrong?"

"Well, yesterday you were being mean and forcing me to marry you and today we are making plans to elope."

"Life is funny."

"No, life is odd. Do you think we are rushing into it, I mean, it's only been two days?"

"Zara, we've already lost enough time, why should we wait. If it wasn't for your brother causing the rift between us and me acting like a dick, we would be married by now."

"Do you think so?"

"I know so. Now, it's time to eat this delicious meal, which hopefully isn't too cold, drink champagne and toast to a happy life together."

"Ok."

He helped her into her seat and poured the champagne before sitting opposite her. "To us."

"To us." She touched her glass to his.

"Hurry up and eat, baby, I can't wait to get you home."

She blushed at the look he sent her way. "I'm nervous." She admitted.

"You have no reason to be. I'm going to worship you. The second time, I'm going to show you how good it can be to go fast."

Her eyes widened, "The second time? I thought men couldn't, you know..." she trailed off.

"Do it twice?" he finished for her. "Zara, I'm confident I will be able to make love to you more than twice, but I don't want to make you sore. You turn me on like no other."

She didn't know what to say to that.

"Pick up your fork and eat," he ordered gently. "The food is delicious and you need your strength."

7 ~ ZARA

Zara lay on Derek's bed completely bare after he'd just spent the last half an hour teasing her and stripping her. Now, he was standing to the side taking off his own clothes. She loved his body; he was breathtakingly beautiful. Her eyes widened as he gripped his boxer shorts and pulled them down his legs.

"Holy crap," She murmured.

"Baby," he said amused. "It will be fine."

"I don't believe you."

"I'm going to get you so worked up you won't even feel it."

She gave him a doubtful look. He was huge.

"Trust me."

Sighing, she tried to relax, but when he climbed onto the bed and knelt between her legs, she couldn't help but tense up again while waiting for his next move. His hands went to her thighs and pushed them open wider.

"You have a beautiful pussy; it's all pink and shiny."

She blushed.

"I bet you taste sweet."

Taste? She wasn't sure she wanted him to do that. Opening her mouth to tell him so, she groaned instead as his tongue touched her button. He rubbed it up and down slowly and then he dipped his tongue into her opening. Her hands gripped his hair as her body arched into his mouth.

"That's it, baby. Let yourself feel."

She did as he said. He kept up his steady pace, keeping her on edge, building up her pleasure until it hit her in a wave so strong she felt like she'd left her body. While she recovered, he caressed her everywhere with his strong fingers, building her pleasure again as if she hadn't just had the greatest orgasm of her life. She heard a crinkle and opened her eyes to see him slipping a condom on.

"Are you ready for me?"

"Oh, yes, I want to feel you inside me."

"That's good because there is nothing I want more than to be inside you."

He moved up the bed and knelt between her legs again, this time she felt him brush his sex over her mound gently and then he positioned himself and pushed inside. Her legs tensed and he rubbed them. "Relax baby."

She tried to do that, and she felt him slip all the way inside her. There had been no pain at all.

"Are you ok?" he asked through clenched teeth.

She nodded, moving her hips slightly. "I feel so full."

He groaned and pulled out of her and slowly pushed back in again. "Does it hurt?"

"No, it feels amazing."

"I'm glad. I love you, Zara."

"I love you too."

He leaned down to kiss her and she could taste herself on him. It felt so erotic. His tongue slipped past her lips and started exploring her mouth. His hips thrust faster and instantly her stomach started doing flips. Her desire rose as he kissed her faster, harder, keeping to the same rhythm as his hips. Zara gripped his shoulders, her nails digging into his skin as her orgasm hit her. She pulled her mouth away from his sucking in a breath before screaming his name. Derek groaned and then his body tensed as he fell on top of her. She rubbed his back in a calming motion while she tried to calm her own breathing down. They stayed like that until he lifted his head. "You were worth the wait."

"I was?"

"No other woman has been in my life since the day you told me you were in love with me."

"No woman at all?"

"No."

She smiled before bursting into tears. He gently separated them and tugged her into his arms. "Why are you crying?"

"I'm just so happy."

"Well, can't you laugh instead? I hate to see you cry."

"I'm sorry, I'll stop." She sniffed. She rubbed her hands over her cheeks and looked up shyly. "Ready for round two?"

He chuckled. "Are you?"

She nodded. "Didn't you say it was going to be fast?"

"Hard and fast. I'll dispose of this." He motioned to the condom he still wore.

"I get the contraception injection."

"Does that mean I don't have to wear a condom?"

"Not if you don't want to."

"What do you want?"

"I want to feel you without a barrier."

"Then you will." He grinned. "I'll be right

back."

"I'll be right here." She promised.

She watched him walk naked to the bathroom and smiled to herself.

In just two days, Zara's life had been turned upside down and she couldn't be happier about it. Finally, her wish had come true, they were going to get married, have a family and live happily ever after, just like she'd always wanted.

"What's that smile for, baby?" Derek asked her as he came back into the room.

"I'm just happy."

He smiled. "Me too, I have a plan to make sure you stay that way."

"As long as you always love me, I'll stay that way."

"No more misunderstandings."

"Or interfering brothers."

"Nothing, but you and me."

"And our babies when we have them."

"A happy family life."

She smiled. "Just what I've always wanted."

THE END

ALSO FROM THE AUTHOR

His Love Series:

Blackmailing his Love (Book One)

Claiming his Love (Book Two)

Protecting his Love (Book Three)

His Love Box Set, Books 1-3

Vampire Love Series:

Her Vampire Love

Her Vampire Mates

Small Town Pack Series:

Jaxon (Book One)

Deacon (Book Two)

Gabe & Mackenzie (Book Three)

The Complete Small Town Pack Series Box Set

Pursuit Series:

Unexpected Pursuit

Reckless Pursuit

Choosing Him Series:

Elle's Choice

The Conclusion

Standalone Titles

Her Mistake

Unlikely Love

Regretful Revenge

Her Second Beginning

Catching Jessa

The Day We Met

Made in the USA
Las Vegas, NV
13 October 2024